UK edition produced for
The Book People,
Hall Wood Avenue,
Haydock,
St Helen's WA11 9UL

Canadian edition produced for
Prospero Books,
a division of Chapters Inc.

Devised and produced by
Tucker Slingsby Ltd,
Berkeley House,
73 Upper Richmond Road,
London SW15 2SZ

Designed by Mick Wells
Colour separations through Printlink International Co.
Printed and bound in Singapore through Printlink International Co.

ISBN 1-85613-357-5

Jan Lewis' NURSERY RHYMES

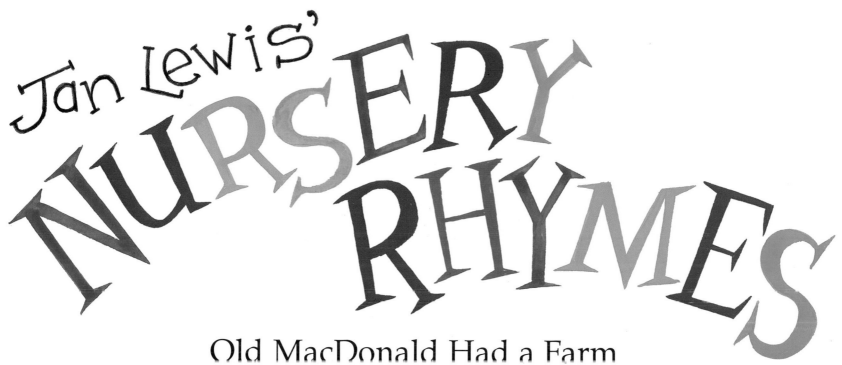

Old MacDonald Had a Farm
One, Two, Buckle My Shoe
Round and Round the Garden
This Little Pig

TED SMART

'Ee-aye-ee

aye - oh !

And on that farm

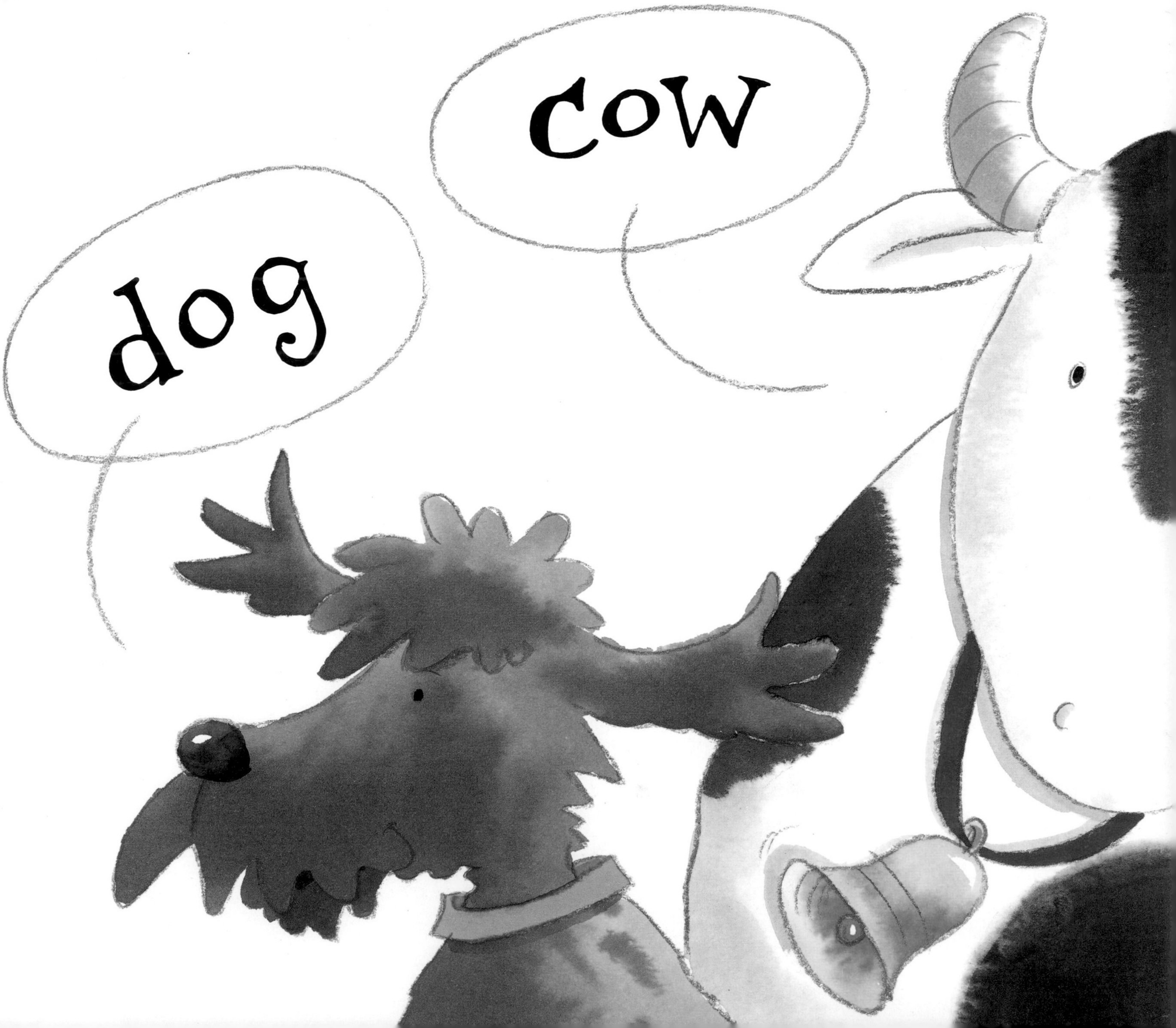

he had a

sheep

duck

aye-oh!

"With a

moo
moo

here...

and a

moo
moo

there.

'And a

Woof
Woof

here...

and a

WOOF
WOOF

there.

'Here a

baa

there a

baa

'Here a

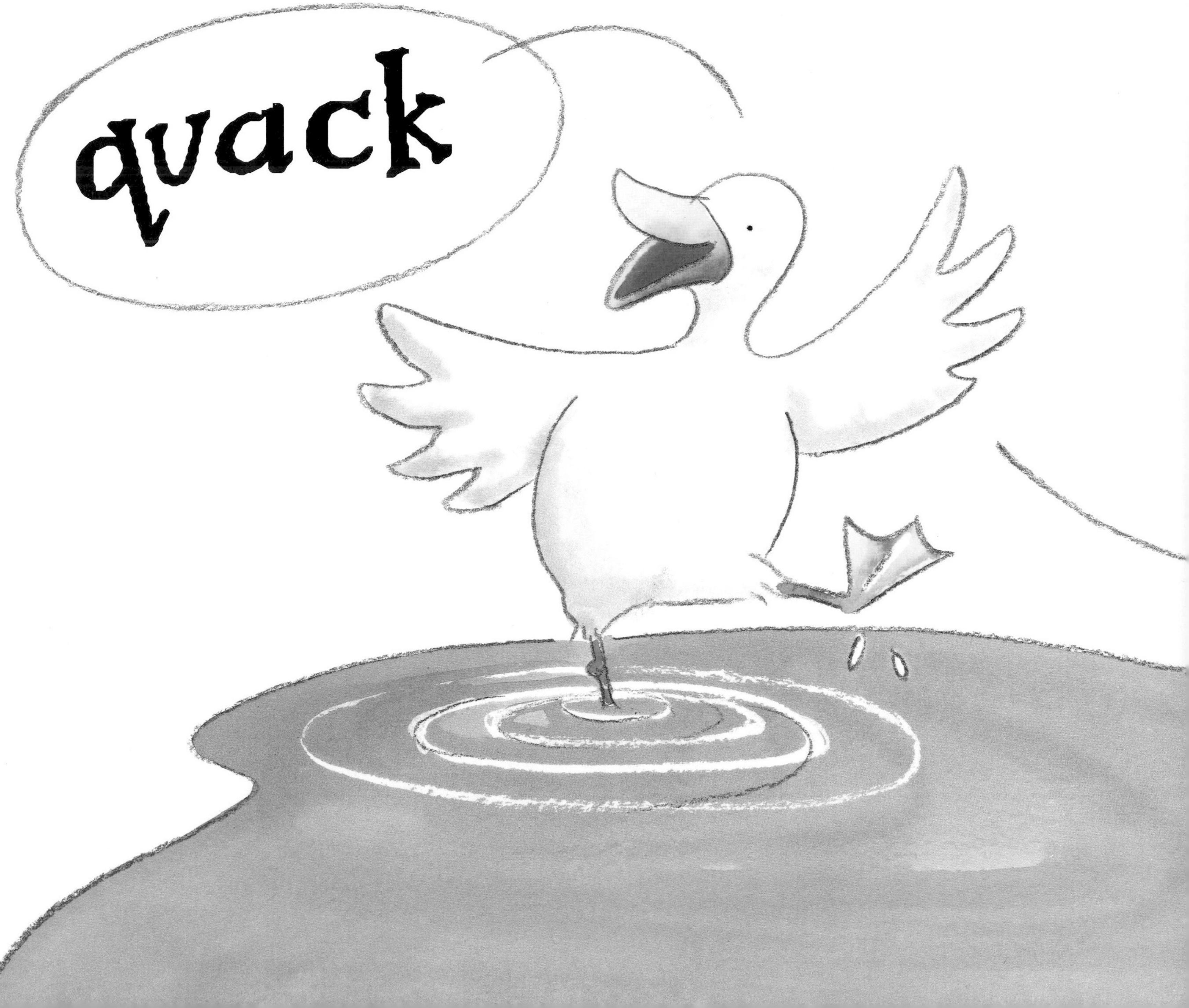

there a

quack

Old Macdonald

Ee-aye-ee –

had a farm, aye-oh!

THE END

ONE, TWO, BUCKLE MY SHOE

One

Two

Three

Four

"Knock at the door.

'Five

Six

Pick up Sticks

Seven

Eight

"Lay them straight."

"Nine

Ten

'A big fat hen!

THE END

ROUND AND ROUND THE GARDEN

'Round and round the garden

'Like a

teddy bear.

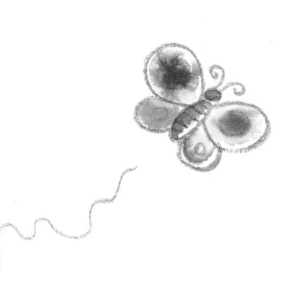

One step

Two steps

'Tickle you

under there!

"Round and round the garden

"In the wind and rain,"

'One
Step

'Two steps

'Tickle you there again!

THE END

THIS LITTLE PIG

This little pig

Went to market.

'This little pig

stayed
at
home.

This little pig

had roast.

beef.

"This little

pig had none.

and this little pig...

...went ee ee eo

all the way home.

THE END

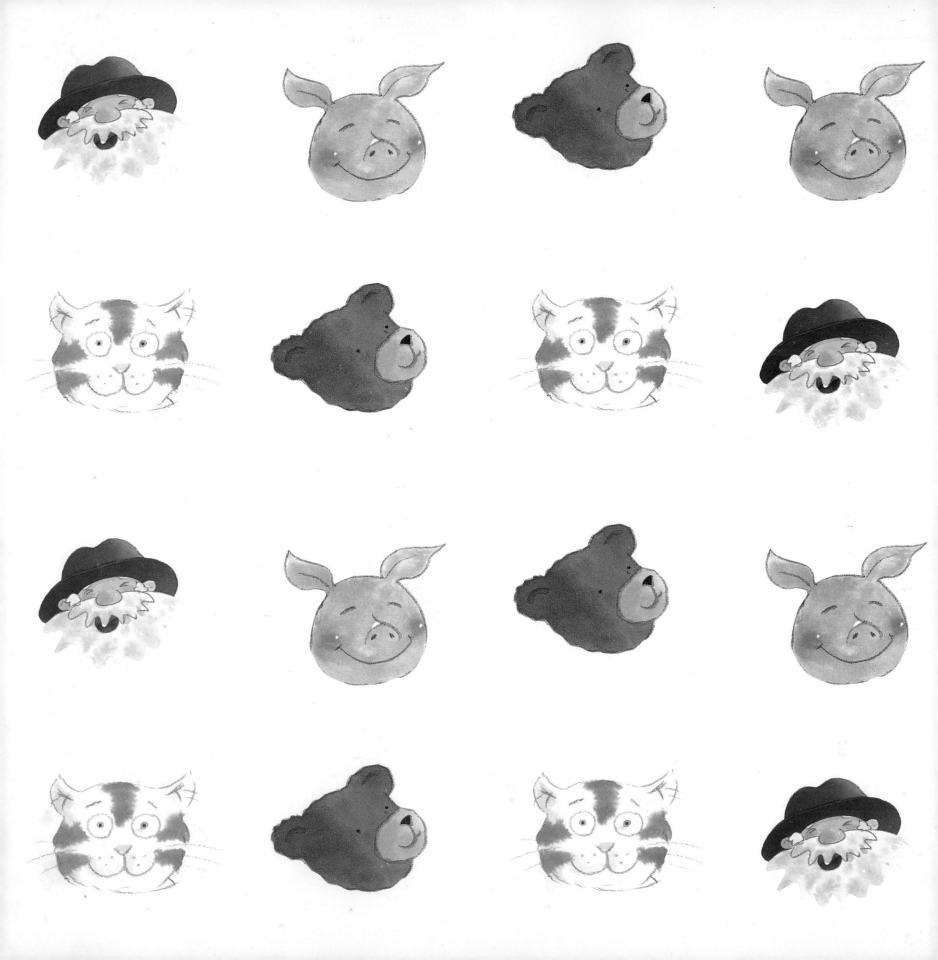